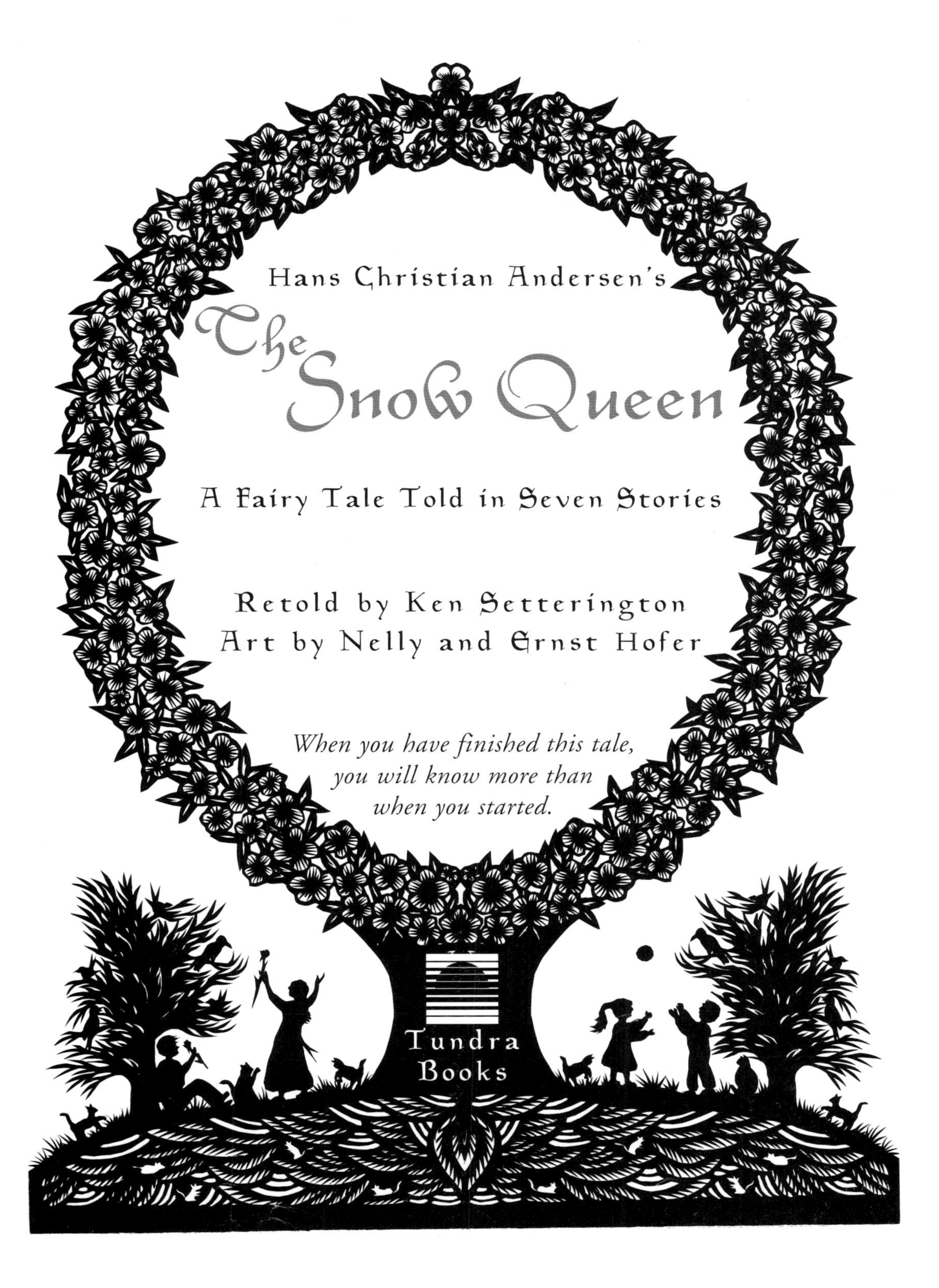

Hans Christian Andersen's

The Snow Queen

A Fairy Tale Told in Seven Stories

Retold by Ken Setterington
Art by Nelly and Ernst Hofer

When you have finished this tale,
you will know more than
when you started.

Tundra Books

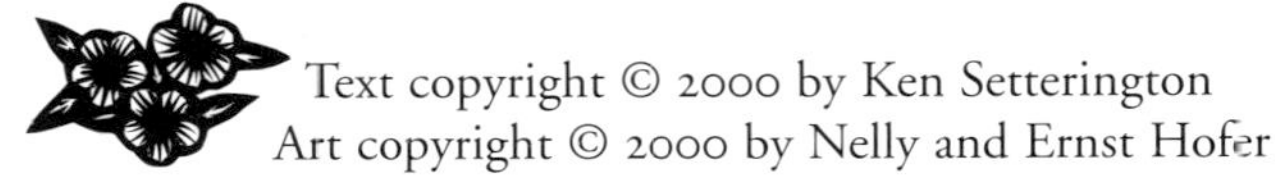

Published in Canada by Tundra Books,
McClelland & Stewart Young Readers,
481 University Avenue, Toronto, Ontario M5G 2E9

Published in the United States by Tundra Books of Northern New York,
P.O. Box 1030, Plattsburgh, New York 12901

Library of Congress Catalog Number: 00-131210

Canadian Cataloguing in Publication Data

Setterington, Ken
Hans Christian Andersen's The snow queen

ISBN 0-88776-497-5

I. Hofer, Nelly. II. Hofer, Ernst, 1961- . III. Andersen, H.C. (Hans Christian), 1805-1875. Snedronningen. IV. Title.

PS8587.E835H36 2000 jC813'.6 C00-930419-3
PZ7.S47Ha 2000

We acknowledge the support of the Canada Council for the Arts and the Ontario Arts Council for our publishing program.

We acknowledge the financial support of the Government of Canada through the Book Publishing Industry Development Program for our publishing activities.

Design by Sari Ginsberg

Printed and bound in Canada

1 2 3 4 5 6 05 04 03 02 01 00

To my parents, who took me to the library as a child, and to the children's librarians I met there.
– K.S.

To our daughter, Jasmin, and our son, Benjamin: We wish you love and happiness on your journey through life.
– N.H. and E.H.

The artists extend sincere appreciation to Kathy Lowinger and the Tundra staff. They would also like to thank Rita Vogt, Bertha Graber, Hedi Graber, and Marie Hofer for helping them make this book possible.

The First Story

The Mirror and Its Fragments

There was once a magician, a particularly evil magician. In fact, he was a demon. He was particularly thrilled with himself for inventing a mirror with strange powers. The mirror could make anything that was good or beautiful look horrid, and all that was evil reflect an attractive appearance. When a kind honorable person looked in the mirror, the reflection was hideous. If that person had a kind thought, then a horrible grin would appear. The mirror would laugh at the kindest people and the magician would laugh at his cleverness. "This is a most amazing and amusing mirror," he would say.

The magician was the headmaster at a school of magic where he told his students that, clearly, he had created a miracle and his mirror reflected the world as it really was. His student magicians ran all over the world with the mirror, showing people their distorted reflections. They so delighted in the horrid images of good and honest people that the students decided to take the mirror up to the heavens to poke fun at the angels. All together they flew to heaven, but as they got close, the mirror laughed harder and harder. In fact, it laughed so hard it shook violently and the student magicians lost their grasp and the mirror fell, breaking into millions of fragments. Those fragments caused more unhappiness. Some of the splinters, tiny as grains of sand, were spread around the world by the wind. When a sliver got into someone's eye, it made him see the world in a most distorted way. If a splinter entered someone's heart, it was even worse – his heart became like a lump of ice. Some pieces of the mirror were large and people used them for windows, giving them a horrible view of the world. Other fragments were made into spectacles, but people who needed to improve their vision were unable to see clearly with them.

The wicked magician was greatly amused with all this and, whenever he thought about his mirror or its fragments, he would laugh until his sides ached.

Some little splinters of the mirror still fly about in the air. And now you will hear about a few of them.

The Second Story

A Little Boy and a Little Girl

In great cities there are so many houses that not all of them can have a garden, not even a little garden. Some families must be satisfied with only a few plants in pots on their window ledges.

There once lived a little boy and a little girl who had a garden a little bit larger than a flowerpot. They weren't brother and sister, but they loved each other as much as if they had been. They lived in attics that were directly across a lane from each other. They could almost reach across from one window to the other because the roof of one house nearly joined the roof of the other. Their grandmothers had window boxes for flowers and kitchen herbs, but instead of placing them right on the window ledges, they placed them across the opening so that a

window-box garden joined their two gables. In each box grew beautiful flowers, and the most magnificent of all were the roses.

In summer, the children would sit in the lane in the shade of the garden and marvel at the roses and flowers that grew above them. In winter, the windows were tightly shut, but the children would heat pennies on the stove and press them on the glass until holes would be melted in the ice. Through these peepholes they could see each other. The little boy was called Kay; the girl's name was Gerda.

When the snow came down hard one winter's day, Kay's grandmother declared, "Those white bees are swarming."

"Do they have a queen bee?" asked Kay, for he knew that real bees have a ruler.

"Ah, yes," said the old woman, "she flies right in the center of the swarm, where the most snowflakes are. She is the biggest, but she never lies down to rest like the other snowflakes do. On winter's nights she flies through the streets and looks in through the windows. Those windows are covered with ice flowers."

"We've seen those!" said the children, and they knew what she said was true.

"Could the Snow Queen come in here?" asked Gerda.

"Let her try," said Kay. "I will put her onto the stove – she will melt."

His grandmother patted his head and told the children another story.

That night as Kay was getting ready for bed, he looked through the peephole in his window and watched the snow fall gently. One snowflake was larger than the rest and it landed right on the window box. It grew and grew, larger and larger, until it became a lady wearing a cape made of millions of snowflakes. She was the most beautiful woman Kay had ever seen, and she was made of glittering ice. Her eyes were like the brightest stars and she beckoned to him with her hand. Kay was frightened and he jumped back from the window. Then a shadow crossed the windowpane as if a big bird was flying by.

The next day there was a clear frost and, soon afterwards, spring arrived – the world turned green. The swallows returned and the windows were opened once again.

That summer the roses bloomed marvelously. As Kay and Gerda sat reading a picture book one afternoon, Kay cried out, "Ouch, ouch! Something has pricked my heart." Then he cried, "Ouch, ouch! Something sharp is in my eye." Gerda looked into his eyes, but there was nothing to be seen.

"I think it is gone," he said, but gone it was not. It was one of the splinters from the mirror. The pain had gone but the splinter remained, and it made everything good appear hateful. Poor Kay also had a splinter in his heart, and his heart grew cold and would soon become like a lump of ice.

"Look," he shouted, "that rose has been gnawed by a worm; it is so ugly. It is almost as ugly as those window boxes." He ran inside and up the stairs to the window boxes and tore out the roses. He laughed at Gerda when she begged him to stop. He called her a baby for reading picture books, and then kicked at the window boxes.

From then on, whenever his grandmother tried to tell him stories, he would argue with her, and whenever anyone came into the house, he would put on her spectacles and mimic her to make them laugh. Soon he could mimic everyone in his lane. People said, "What a joker that boy is." It was the splinters of mirror in his eye and heart that let him hurt everyone, including his friend Gerda. Poor little Gerda, she loved him with all her heart. . . .

Kay did not play as he used to; he now played only with the other boys. One winter's day he called to Gerda to show her snowflakes under a magnifying glass. "These are perfect, much prettier than flowers," he said. Gerda hoped to play with him, but he shouted in her ear, "I am going to the city square with my sled," and then, with a smile, he added, "and *you* can't come." Away he went.

In the square the most daring boys would tie their sleds to farmers' wagons and ride behind as long as they could. Kay, however, managed to tie his sled to the back of a magnificent

white one, with a driver dressed in a white fur hat and coat. They circled the square twice and then departed, traveling faster and faster. Soon they passed the city gates, and the snow began to fall so heavily that Kay could not see anything in front of him. He untied his sled, but it still followed the large white one as if pulled by magic. Kay wanted to pray, but he couldn't remember how. He called out, but no one heard him. The snowflakes seemed larger and larger; it grew colder and colder. At last the big sled stopped and its driver stood up and turned around to look at Kay. The fur hat and coat were made of snow; the driver was a woman. She stood tall and straight. She was beautiful, her eyes like cold stars in the night sky. She was the Snow Queen!

"We have driven fast, but no one likes to be frozen, so come up here and crawl under my bearskin."

Kay climbed up into the big sled and crawled under. He felt like he had fallen into a snowdrift.

"Are you still cold?" she asked, and kissed his forehead. The kiss was colder than ice. It went to his heart, which was half frozen from the journey. At first he thought he would die, but it hurt for only a minute, then he no longer felt the cold.

"My sled, don't forget my sled." They fastened it to the back of the large sled and the Snow Queen kissed Kay again. He

forgot entirely about little Gerda, his grandmother, and his home.

"Now you must not have any more kisses," she said with her cold smile, "or I might kiss you to death."

Kay looked at the Snow Queen. She was so beautiful, he could not imagine that anyone could have a more lovely face. To him, she was utterly perfect. He no longer felt any fear. He told her what he had learned at school, but somehow it seemed that he really didn't know very much. Still the Snow Queen smiled at him, and their sled flew high into the black storm clouds above the earth. When daylight came, Kay fell asleep at the feet of the Snow Queen.

The Third Story

The Enchanted Flower Garden

How did little Gerda fare when Kay did not return? Where could he have gone? No one knew. The boys in the square reported that he had tied his sled to a resplendent white one and had raced through the streets, but that was all they knew. Others said that he may have drowned in the river that ran through the city. Gerda cried long and bitterly. It was a long and bitter winter.

Finally spring came with the warmth of the sunlight.

"Kay is dead and gone," said little Gerda.

"We don't believe that," the sunbeams replied.

"Neither do we," said the sparrows.

Gerda wondered what she could do, or whom she could ask. She decided to put on her new red shoes, go to the river, and ask after him.

"Is it true you have taken my friend?" she said to the river. "I will give you my red shoes if you will give him back to me."

The waves seemed to nod strangely. So she took off her shoes and threw them into the river, but the waves brought them quickly back. It was as if the river wouldn't take the shoes because it hadn't taken Kay, but Gerda thought she had not thrown the shoes out far enough. A rowboat was close by, so Gerda climbed in, scurried to the farthest point, and threw her shoes as hard as she could. The boat wasn't fastened to the shore and it began to drift. Gerda turned quickly, but the boat was too far out and she didn't dare jump. The boat floated faster and faster downstream with the current. Little Gerda started to cry, but then wondered if the river was taking her to Kay. She took great comfort in that thought, and for hours watched the beautiful landscape drift by.

Soon the boat passed a cottage in a cherry orchard, with two wooden soldiers standing in front. Not knowing they were made of wood, Gerda called loudly to them, thinking they could help her. But an old woman came out of the house and saw poor little Gerda floating by. She was wearing a large hat with the most beautiful flowers painted on it, and she was walking with a shepherd's crook. Rushing to the water's edge, she caught hold of the boat with her crook and pulled Gerda to shore.

"Poor child. What a long way the river has carried you."

Gerda, glad to be on dry land, looked with uncertainty at the strange old woman.

"Tell me who you are and how you got here," said the old woman as she led her through her garden.

Gerda told her everything and asked if she had seen little Kay. The old woman said no, but that he would surely come soon and that, in the meantime, Gerda should eat some cherries and enjoy the flowers. Her flowers were prettier than any picture book and each one could tell a story. She took Gerda into her cottage, where a large bowl of cherries sat on a table in the center of the room. While Gerda ate the cherries, the old woman combed her hair. "Oh, I have longed for a little girl like you. What good friends we shall be." Gerda thought less and less of Kay while her hair was being combed.

Although the old woman knew witchcraft, she wasn't an evil witch; she just liked to do a little magic for her own pleasure. Now she wanted to keep little Gerda very much. She ran to the garden with her crook and pointed it at her rosebushes, sinking them into the dark earth. She was afraid that if Gerda saw the roses, she would be reminded of Kay.

Gerda followed the old woman into the garden. What a magnificent garden it was! Every flower of every season was there in full bloom. Gerda played among the flowers till the sun set behind the tall cherry trees. That night she was given the loveliest of beds, with a crimson quilt stuffed with violet leaves. She slept with deep sweet dreams.

The next day, and for many days, she played in the sunshine with the flowers and soon she knew the garden well. She sensed that there was something missing, but she couldn't think what it might be. Then one day she looked at the old woman's grand hat with the wonderful painted flowers and saw a rose. The old woman had forgotten about the rose on her hat.

"What!" cried Greta. "Aren't there any roses in this garden?" She ran from one flower bed to another, searching and searching, but there weren't any roses. She felt so sad that she sat down and wept. Her tears landed on the very plot of land where a rose-bush had once grown. They moistened the ground and, at once, the bush shot up anew and blossomed triumphantly. Gerda kissed the flowers, thinking of the roses at home and of Kay.

"I have stayed here too long!" she cried. "I left home to search for Kay. Do you know where he is? Is he dead?" she asked the roses.

"Dead he is not," they answered. "We have been under the ground where the dead lie and he is not there."

"Oh, thank you," said Gerda and she went to the other flowers and asked them if they knew where Kay was. Each flower wanted to tell its own tale. Their stories were wondrous, replete with strange and exotic people and places, but none of the flowers knew anything about Kay. When she realized that none of them could tell her where to find him, Gerda tied up her long dress and ran to the end of the garden.

The gate was shut, but she pushed on the door with all her might. The old rusty latch gave way and the gate sprang open. With bare feet, little Gerda ran out into the wide world. Three times she looked back, but no one seemed to be following her.

She ran as far as she could and, when she could run no farther, she stopped to catch her breath. Sitting on a large stone, she looked around and realized that it was autumn. It had always been summer inside the garden, but outside it was now close to winter.

"There is no time to lose; I have wasted so much time already," sighed Gerda, and she got up and walked on. Her little feet were cold and tired as she passed a willow tree with its yellowing leaves. How cold and gray the wide world seemed!

The Fourth Story

The Prince and the Princess

Gerda was obliged to stop and rest and, while she stood in the snow, a large raven flew down and stopped in front of her. "Caw, caw, good day, good day." He watched her carefully, and then asked where she was going all alone. Gerda told the raven her story and asked if he had seen Kay.

The raven nodded his head thoughtfully and said, "I may have. It is possible."

"Oh, he is alive!" said Gerda. She kissed the raven and, in her joy, almost hugged him to death.

"Gently, gently," said the raven. "I think I have seen Kay, but if it is Kay, then he has forgotten you for a princess."

"A princess? Does he live with a princess?"

The raven then told her all that he had heard.

In the kingdom where they were standing, there lived a clever princess who read all the newspapers in the world. One day she decided to marry, but only if she could find a man who knew what to say when people spoke to him, not just one who could look grand. (The raven knew all about this, for he had a tame sweetheart who hopped freely about the palace.) The princess announced she would choose the young man for her husband who showed himself to be most at home in the palace.

The raven looked at Gerda, "What I say is true; you can believe this. The men came in droves. They could speak well enough outside the palace, but once they got inside and saw the royal guards, the golden staircase, the magnificent ballroom, they became quite overwhelmed. When the princess spoke to them, they could repeat only what she had just said. It was as if they had been struck dumb the moment they entered the palace."

"But what of Kay . . . when did he come?" asked Gerda.

"I was just getting to him. On the third day there came a youth. He didn't have a horse or carriage; his clothes were shabby and his eyes sparkled."

"That was Kay," she said, clapping her hands with joy.

"He carried a knapsack on his back."

"No, not a knapsack, but a sled. He had a sled when he left home."

"It is possible," answered the raven. "When he entered the palace and saw the guards, he nodded to them and said, 'It must be very boring standing here.' He walked into the rooms, all ablaze with light. My sweetheart told me that his boots creaked with every step he took."

"Oh, yes, most certainly that was Kay. I know he had new boots. I remember them creaking."

"They really did creak, but he went boldly up to the princess, who was sitting upon a huge pearl with all of her maids of honor and gentlemen-in-waiting."

"Did Kay win the princess?"

"The young man spoke as well as I do when I use my raven tongue – at least that is what my sweetheart said. The young man said he had not come to woo her, but only to hear her wisdom. She liked him very much and he liked her in return."

"Oh, yes, to be sure that was Kay," said Gerda. "Oh, will you take me into the palace?"

"Ah, that is easily asked," replied the raven, "but it is not easy to get permission for a girl to enter the palace – especially a girl without shoes, like you. But wait here by the trellis and I will talk it over with my sweetheart. I am sure she will know what to do."

The raven did not return until late evening. "Caw, caw," he said. "My sweetheart sends you this piece of bread; she thought you might be hungry. You would never be allowed to enter the palace looking like you do, but my sweetheart knows a little back staircase that leads to the sleeping apartments and she knows where the key is kept."

So they went through the town until they came to a back door that stood half open. Gerda's heart trembled with fear and longing. She was afraid that she was doing something wrong, yet she only wished to know if Kay was there. How glad he would be to see her! They went up the back staircase and, at the top, came upon a lamp burning and a tame raven standing in the middle of the floor. Gerda curtsied, as her grandmother had taught her.

"My fiancé has told me all about you. Your adventures sound so exciting," said the tame raven. "Now, if you would take the lamp, I will show you the way."

Unlocking a door with the key, they went through room after room, each one more beautiful than the last. When they reached the royal bedchamber, Gerda was amazed. The ceiling was covered with crystal, and two beds hung from a golden tree. They looked like lilies. One was white and in it lay the princess. The other was red and in this one Gerda sought her playmate. She bent aside the red leaves and saw a little tanned neck. Oh, it must be Kay! She called his name and held the lamp up high. He awoke and turned his head, but it was not Kay.

The princess looked out from her lily-white bed and asked what the matter was. Then little Gerda wept and told her story and about how the ravens had helped her. The prince and princess tried to comfort her, and they praised the ravens. The prince gave Gerda his bed and encouraged her to sleep.

The next day she was dressed from head to toe in silk and velvet. They invited her to stay in the palace, but Gerda begged for only a small carriage, a horse, and a pair of boots. She just wanted to go out into the wide world to seek Kay.

They gave her boots, warm clothes, and a muff. As soon as Gerda was ready to leave, a fine carriage of the purest gold drove up in front of the castle. Not only did she have a coachman, but also a footman and two outriders. The prince and princess helped her into the coach and gave her sugarplums, fruit, and gingerbread. The first raven she had met decided to ride with her for the first few miles.

"Farewell! Farewell!" cried the prince and princess. Gerda wept, for she had grown so fond of them, and the raven wept in sympathy. After a few miles the raven flew out the carriage window, and that was harder still. He flew up to a tree branch and flapped his wings at the carriage until it drove out of sight.

The Fifth Story

The Little Robber-Girl

"Gold," shouted the robbers when they saw the coach approaching, "it is gold!" They rushed and grabbed the horses, killed the coachman, the footman, and the outriders, and dragged little Gerda out of the coach.

"She is nice and plump; I'll bet she has been fed on nuts and fruits," said the old robber-wife as she squeezed Gerda's arm. "She will taste just like a nice fattened lamb." She took a long fearsome knife out of her belt. But she then shrieked, "Oh, oh, stop," for at that moment her daughter had jumped up onto her back and bitten her ear.

"She will play with me. She will give me her muff and her pretty dress, and she will sleep with me," declared the robber-girl and, just to be sure that her mother understood, she bit her ear again.

The robber-girl was a spoilt child. She climbed into the carriage with Gerda, took her muff and put her hands into it. "Don't worry. She won't kill you as long as I love you! Are you a princess?"

Gerda then told her all that had happened and how much she loved Kay. The robber-girl looked at her seriously and then

said that she would never allow anyone to kill her; in fact, if she got annoyed with her, she would kill her herself.

At last the coach reached the robbers' castle. It was half ruined, and large dogs ran about looking as if they could eat humans. The girls entered a vast smoky hall where a cauldron of soup was bubbling. The robber-girl led Gerda to the far end where there were some blankets on a pile of straw. Wood pigeons and doves were nesting all around them. "These all belong to me," said the robber-girl and she grabbed a frightened bird by the feet and shoved it in Gerda's face. "Kiss it," she said and started to laugh. She then showed Gerda a reindeer that was tied to a large stone. "We have to tie him up, or else he will run away. Besides, I tickle him every evening with my dagger – it makes him afraid of me." She then took out her own dagger from a crack in the wall and ran the sharp point over the reindeer's neck. The animal struggled and tried to back away, but the robber-girl just laughed. Still laughing, she pulled Gerda down onto the blankets with her.

"Do you always sleep with your knife?" asked frightened Gerda.

"Yes, of course. One never knows what might happen," she replied, but then asked Gerda to tell her about Kay and how she came to be in the world all by herself.

Gerda told her story again and the wood pigeons cooed. The little robber-girl threw one arm around Gerda's neck, grasped her dagger with the other, and soon fell fast asleep. But little Gerda couldn't sleep – she wondered what would happen to her and, besides, the little robber-girl snored terribly.

One of the wood pigeons cooed to her, "We have seen little Kay. He rode in the white sled of the Snow Queen. She rode by our nest in the woods and breathed on us – all the young ones died."

"Where was she going?" asked Gerda.

"She was most likely traveling to Lapland, where there is always snow and ice. Ask the reindeer."

"Lapland," said the reindeer, "is a glorious place. The Snow Queen has her summer tent there, but her palace is further north, close to the North Pole."

"Oh, my poor dear Kay!" mumbled Gerda. The little robber-girl mumbled a *shhhhh* and Gerda, remembering the dagger, was quiet.

In the morning Gerda told the robber-girl what the pigeons and the reindeer had told her. The robber-girl looked grave and asked the reindeer if he knew where Lapland was. "Of course," was his reply. "I was born there; I used to love to run over the icy plains."

The little robber-girl grabbed Gerda's hand and said, "All the men are out, but my mother is still here. She will stay here all day, but after her noon meal she will take a nap. I will do something for you then."

After the robber-wife ate at noon, she lay down and was soon snoring very loudly. The robber-girl went over to the reindeer and laughed, "I like tickling you with this knife and I will miss it, but now I will untie you if you agree to take this girl to Lapland as fast as you can." The reindeer jumped for joy and Gerda was helped up onto his back. "Here are your boots," the robber-girl added. "You will need them, but I will keep your muff because it is so pretty – but wait, you needn't be cold!" She ran and took her mother's large gloves and gave them to Gerda.

Gerda, in her joy, began to cry.

"Stop that; I don't like crying. You should be glad you will soon find your friend." The robber-girl then gave Gerda two loaves of bread and some ham. She led the reindeer to the door of the ruined castle and, as soon as they departed, called out after them, "Run, run and take care of each other."

Gerda waved with her huge gloves and the reindeer ran. They traveled through forests and across great plains, over moors and meadows. It seemed one night that the sky had burst and the most brilliant colors filled the darkness. "Ah, my dear Northern Lights," said the reindeer and he ran even faster. When the loaves and the ham were eaten, they had reached Lapland.

The Sixth Story

The Lapp Woman and the Finn Woman

Gerda could hardly believe that they had reached a little hut. The roof nearly touched the ground and they had to crawl to go inside. The only one there was an old Lapp woman, who was busy boiling fish. Gerda was so cold she couldn't speak, so the reindeer told the old woman Gerda's story, but only after he had told his own, which he felt was much more important.

"Oh, you poor dear," said the Lapp woman to Gerda. "You still have a hundred miles to go before you reach Finland. The Snow Queen is there now – she shoots off blue fireworks every night. I will send you to a wise Finn woman who knows more about the Snow Queen than I do. I have no paper, but I will send a message on a dried fish."

When Gerda was warm and had eaten her fill, it was time to be on her way again. She took the dried codfish with the message and rode away on the reindeer at full speed.

The beautiful blue Northern Lights shone brightly as they rode. When they reached Finland, they found the wise woman's hut. It was so small that at first they couldn't find the door, so they knocked on the chimney. They crept inside, and was it ever hot! The wise woman wore hardly any clothes at all, and at once helped Gerda take off a few of her garments so the heat would be bearable. She then took a large piece of ice and put it on the reindeer's head. Sitting down, she read what had been written on the codfish. She read the message three times and then tossed the fish into the pot that was boiling over the fire. "No sense in wasting anything," her eyes seemed to say. The reindeer told his story and then told Gerda's. The wise woman squinted her eyes and was lost in deep thought.

"Could you make a potion to give Gerda the strength of twelve men? Then she could overcome the Snow Queen," asked the reindeer.

"The strength of twelve men is of no use." The wise woman took the reindeer aside and whispered to him, "Little Kay is with the Snow Queen and he finds everything just fine. He has a glass splinter in his heart and another in his eye. The Snow Queen will always have power over him as long as he has those splinters."

"Can't you give Gerda something to help her remove those pieces of glass?"

"She already has a great power. Men and animals serve her. How else could she have come so far? She has a pure and loving heart and, with that power, she can enter the Snow Queen's palace and free Kay. There is nothing greater that I can give her. Two miles from here is the Snow Queen's garden. Take her there now and leave her near the bush with the red berries. Don't waste time and come right back." The wise woman lifted Gerda onto the back of the reindeer and urged them on.

"Oh, I forgot my boots and my gloves!" cried Gerda, but the reindeer dared not stop. He ran until he reached the garden and found the snow-covered bush with the red berries peaking out. He set her down and kissed her. Tears rolled down his face, but he turned and raced back to the wise woman.

There stood Gerda in the arctic cold, without boots or gloves. She ran as fast as she could, but her way was blocked with snowflakes. It wasn't snowing – the sky was clear and bright – yet as Gerda ran farther, the snowflakes got bigger and bigger. Gerda remembered how they had appeared when she looked through the magnifying glass. They had been beautiful, but now they were blocking her way. She realized that they were the Snow Queen's guards.

Gerda prayed as she ran. She could see her breath and it seemed to grow thicker. Angels rose from its warmth and hovered all around her. Each wore a helmet and carried a spear. They thrust the spears into the snowflakes, breaking them into thousands of pieces. Then the angels rubbed Gerda's feet and hands until she didn't feel the cold.

But what was Kay doing? He certainly was not thinking of Gerda, and he would never have imagined that she was standing right outside the Snow Queen's palace.

The Seventh Story

The Snow Queen's Palace

The walls of the palace were made of snow, and the doors and windows were the sharp winds. There were hundreds of rooms and some were miles in length. They were all a dazzling white, empty and cold, all lit by the Northern Lights. In the very center of the palace was a frozen lake. It had cracked into thousands of pieces and each piece was identical. When the Snow Queen was at home, her throne was in the very center of the lake. She called the lake her mirror and declared it to be the finest mirror in the world.

Little Kay was almost black-and-blue with cold, but he couldn't feel it. The Snow Queen had kissed all his feeling of cold away. His heart was already a lump of ice and he was busy with the ice fragments from the frozen lake, trying to put a word together. The Snow Queen had promised him that he would be his own master if he could put together the word "eternity," but Kay could never remember the word. He sat with the ice fragments like a child playing with building blocks or a puzzle.

The Snow Queen had just left to visit the warmer countries and see the volcanoes. She liked to whiten the peaks of their black craters. She had left Kay sitting all alone in the great empty hall of ice.

The winds blew terribly as Gerda entered the palace gates, but they died down when they heard her prayers. She entered the great hall and saw Kay. She knew him right away. "Kay, Kay, at last I have found you!" She hugged him with great joy, but little Kay sat cold and stiff. Gerda burst into tears. Her hot tears fell on his chest and the warmth thawed his heart. Gerda looked at him, begging him to remember their little garden with the roses and how they had bloomed each summer. Then Kay's tears burst forth and he cried so much that the splinter of glass washed from his eye.

"Gerda, Gerda, my own dear Gerda, where have you been?" He looked around and asked, "Where have I been? How cold it is here." Gerda was laughing and crying at the same time, but Kay picked her up and danced with her. The pieces of ice joined in the dance and the hall was filled with joy. When Gerda and Kay grew tired and stopped dancing, the ice fragments fell, forming the word "eternity."

Gerda kissed Kay's cheeks, his eyes, his hands and feet. His true color came back and his eyes sparkled. He was healthy and happy once again. The Snow Queen might return, but it wouldn't matter – Kay's freedom was written on the lake in the word "eternity."

Gerda and Kay took each other by the hand and left the Snow Queen's palace. The sun burst forth and the winds turned calm. The reindeer was waiting for them by the bush with the red berries. He had brought another reindeer, with udders full of warm milk. After the children had drunk their fill, they rode off to the Finn woman, who gave them a meal of boiled codfish. They then traveled to the house of the Lapp woman who had given them warm food. They all rode in her sled to the border of Lapland, but then green grass started to poke through the snow and the sled could go no farther. "Farewell, farewell," each one said, and the reindeer and the Lapp woman returned to Lapland.

Hand in hand Gerda and Kay wandered on until they heard the most glorious sound. It was birds – they had not heard birds for many a long day. Through the forest a horse came galloping towards them. Gerda recognized the horse as it had once pulled her gold coach. Suddenly she realized that the rider was the robber-girl – she was delighted to see them and told how she had left her home in the forest and was off to other parts of the world. She looked at Kay closely and said, "You are a fine one, running off to the end of the earth. I wonder if you are worth Gerda's trip?"

Gerda only smiled and asked about the prince, the princess, and the ravens. The royal couple were traveling in foreign countries, and the robber-girl then told about the raven's death and his tame sweetheart hopping about the palace with a piece of black wool tied to her leg. "But tell me how you got Kay," she said.

Gerda and Kay told their story and the robber-girl declared that the ending was just as exciting as the beginning. She promised that if she ever visited their city, she would surely come to see them. She jumped back onto her horse, put her dagger in her belt, and rode off into the wide world.

Spring, with its bright flowers and green grass, greeted Gerda and Kay as they continued their journey. They came to a city where church bells were ringing, and they knew at once that they were home. In no time at all they were climbing the steps up to Kay's grandmother's apartment. Hand in hand they went to the window and looked out at their window-box garden. The roses were in bloom; they sat on their own little stools and gazed at their beauty. The icy splendor of the Snow Queen's palace vanished like a forgotten dream.

Author's Note

The illustrations in *The Snow Queen* have been created using sharp, tiny-bladed scissors and very careful hands. *Scherenschnitt* – the German word for silhouette – is an art that is believed to have originated in Asia centuries ago. In China, pictures were created by cutting a single piece of parchment with a knife.

The technique of paper cutting was brought to Europe by travelers from Asia by the end of the seventeenth century, and the art form quickly flourished. In France, it became fashionable to have portraits created using cut-paper, instead of commissioning expensive oil paintings. These portraits were called silhouettes after the French finance minister Etienne de Silhouette, known for his economy. By the time Hans Christian Andersen was writing his fairy tales in the nineteenth century, paper cutting was a very popular art form.

Hans Christian Andersen enjoyed the art of paper cutting and was well known for his fantastic paper creations. Not only did he write and tell his own stories, but he also accompanied them with intricate paper cuts, many of which he shared with children.

As the art of photography developed, the public turned from the cut-paper silhouette to the photograph to capture their likeness. Hans Christian Andersen was one of the early proponents of photography. Fascinated by both the technology and the art form, he had a vast number of portraits taken of himself. As photography grew in popularity and silhouettes became less fashionable, paper cutting was used more as a decorative art.

The *scherenschnitte* in this book are evidence of the fantastic images that can be created with paper and scissors, which are, as an art form, still cherished today.

Hans Christian Andersen
1805 – 1875